PIGGIES ✦ PIGGIES ✦ PIGGIES

A Treasury of Stories, Songs, & Poems

Compiled by Walter Retan

Illustrated by S. D. Schindler and other illustrators

SIMON & SCHUSTER BOOKS FOR YOUNG READERS

PUBLISHED BY SIMON & SCHUSTER

NEW YORK   LONDON   TORONTO   SYDNEY   TOKYO   SINGAPORE

SIMON & SCHUSTER BOOKS FOR YOUNG READERS
Simon & Schuster Building
Rockefeller Center
1230 Avenue of the Americas
New York, NY 10020
Copyright © 1993 by Parachute Press, Inc.
All rights reserved including the right of reproduction in whole or in part in any form.
SIMON & SCHUSTER BOOKS FOR YOUNG READERS is a trademark of
Simon & Schuster.
Designed by Michel Design
Manufactured in the United States of America
10 9 8 7 6 5 4 3 2 1

Library of Congress Cataloging-in-Publication Data

Piggies, piggies, piggies / compiled by Walter Retan; illustrated by Steven Schindler and other illustrators.
    p. cm.
    Summary: A collection of stories, poems, songs, and games about pigs, by such authors as E. B. White and Beatrix Potter.
    1. Swine—Literary collections. [1. Pigs—Literary collections.]
    I. Retan, Walter. II. Schindler, S. D., ill.
PZ5.P618 1992   91-34665
808.8'036—dc20   CIP

ISBN: 0-671-75244-8

ACKNOWLEDGMENTS

Every effort has been made to trace the ownership of all copyrighted material and to secure the necessary permissions to reprint these selections. If any question arises as to the use of any material, the editor and the publisher, while expressing regret for any inadvertent error, will make the necessary correction in future printings.

Grateful acknowledgment is made to the following for permission to reprint copyrighted material:

Bantam Doubleday Dell Publishing Group, Inc. for "Mary Middling," from *Fifty-One New Nursery Rhymes* by Rose Fyleman, copyright © 1931, 1932 by Doubleday, a division of Bantam Doubleday Dell Publishing Group, Inc. Used by permission of Doubleday, a division of Bantam Doubleday Dell Publishing Group, Inc.; HarperCollins for U.S. and Canadian rights to *Poinsettia & Her Family* by Felicia Bond, text and illustrations copyright © 1981 by Felicia Bond; "There Was a Small Pig Who Wept Tears" and "There Was a Light Pig From Montclair" from *The Book of Pigericks (Pig Limericks)* by Arnold Lobel, text and illustrations copyright © 1983 by Arnold Lobel; "Wilbur's Boast" from *Charlotte's Web*, by E. B. White, text and illustrations copyright 1952 by E. B. White renewed © 1980 by E. B. White; Ludlow Music, Inc., for "Tale of a Little Pig" (Tale of Five Little Pigs), collected, adapted, and arranged by Alan Lomax and John A. Lomax, copyright © 1934 (renewed); McIntosh and Otis, Inc. for "The Jokes of Single-Toe" from *Padre Porko* by Robert Davis, copyright © 1939, 1948 by Robert Davis; Penguin USA for "The Very Long Trip" from *Tales of Amanda Pig* by Jean Van Leeuwen, copyright © 1983 by Jean Van Leeuwen for text. Used by permission of Dial Books for Young Readers, a division of Penguin Books USA Inc; Gareth Reeves for "A Pig Tale" from *The Blackbird in the Lilac* by James Reeves; Frederick Warne & Co. for illustrations from *The Tale of Pigling Bland*, by Beatrix Potter copyright © 1913, 1987.

Illustrations on pages 40 and 41 by Diane de Groat.
Illustrations on pages 42, 43, 58, and 59 by Kees deKiefte.
Illustrations on pages 22, 23, 70, 71, and 96 by Marlene Ekman.
Illustrations on pages 10, 11, 32, and 33 by Benrei Huang.
Illustrations on pages 8, 9, 20, and 21 by Kathy Wilburn.

Contents

To the Reader

t's fun to watch young farm pigs. They are plump, friendly, and intelligent, and they can run very fast on their short little legs. If you've ever tried to catch one, you know! Pigs will also eat more than they should—as I learned when I was a child.

I was visiting a friend of mine on a farm, and he took me to a shed to see a family of piglets. Pointing to a nearby pile of apples, Tom told me that the pigs loved them. So we started throwing apples into their pen. The pigs gobbled them up as fast as we threw them in. In fact, they didn't stop eating—and we didn't stop throwing—until every single apple had disappeared.

That evening at the dinner table, Tom's father looked at us sternly and asked, "Did you feed all those apples to the pigs?" We nodded, knowing right away that something was wrong.

"Well," he said, "the pigs have been sick all afternoon. You should have known better than to do that." We were in disgrace. But worse yet was the knowledge that we had made those cute little piglets sick. Fortunately, they recovered fast, and you can be sure that we never gave them any more apples.

Although pigs do have big appetites, their reputation for being dirty animals is undeserved. Actually they are very clean. The problem is that their sweat glands don't do a good job of keeping them cool. So, on hot summer days, they love to roll in the mud, which cools them off. When they are in a neat, cool stall, they keep themselves very clean.

Pigs are smart animals. You can even teach them tricks—just as the young swineherds do in "Pigs and Pirates," an old folktale retold in this book. Perhaps because they are both cute and clever, pigs have been favorite characters in folktales and children's books for hundreds of years. One of the first stories that English-speaking children hear is "The Three Little Pigs." They love to huff and puff—right along with the wicked wolf—and they scream with delight if the storyteller tickles them under the chin when repeating, "Not by the hair of my chinny chin chin."

Many popular Mother Goose rhymes are about pigs. "This Little Piggy Went to Market," "Barber, Barber, Shave a Pig," and "Little Jack Sprat" are just three. In addition, such well-known poets as Christina Rossetti, James Reeves, and Rose Fyleman have written amusing poems celebrating pigs. There are also many enchanting stories by such renowned authors as E. B. White (*Charlotte's Web*), Jean Van Leeuwen (*Tales of Amanda Pig*), and Beatrix Potter (*The Tale of Pigling Bland*).

In *Piggies, Piggies, Piggies*, you will find a wonderful selection of all these poems, songs, games, and stories, accompanied by colorful illustrations from such classic illustrators as Garth Williams, Beatrix Potter, and Arnold Lobel.

W. R.

Dickery, Dickery, Dare

Dickery, dickery, dare,
The pig flew up in the air;
The man in brown soon brought him down,
Dickery, dickery, dare.

Little Jack Sprat

Little Jack Sprat
Once had a pig;
It was not very little,
Nor yet very big,
It was not very lean,
It was not very fat—
"It's a good pig to grunt,"
Said little Jack Sprat.

Barber, Barber

Barber, barber, shave a pig,
How many hairs to make a wig?
Four and twenty, that's enough,
Give the barber a pinch of snuff.

This Little Pig-a-Wig

This little pig had a rub-a-dub,
This little pig had a scrub-a-scrub,
This little pig-a-wig ran upstairs,
This little pig-a-wig called out, Bears!
Down came the jar with a loud
    Slam! Slam!
And this little pig had all the jam.

Piggy on the Railway

Piggy on the railway,
Picking up stones;
Make fist with right hand.

Along came an engine
And broke poor Piggy's bones.
Make fist with left hand.
Move left fist toward
right fist until they touch.

"Oh!" said Piggy,
"That's not fair."
Shake one finger from right fist.

"Oh!" said the engine driver,
"I don't care!"
Shrug shoulders.

Little Piggy-Wig on the Farm Close By

Little piggy-wig on the farm close by,
All by himself ran away from the sty.
*Move index finger and middle finger
back and forth along the floor.*

The dog said, "Woof."
The cow said, "Moo."
The sheep said, "Baa."
The dove said, "Coo."
Make the sounds of the animals.

Little piggy-wig began to cry,
And as fast as he could he ran back to the sty.
*Move index finger and middle finger
back and forth along the floor.*

11

This Little Piggy Went to Market

illustrations by Julie Durrell

This little ⬤ went to 🏪

This little ⬤ stayed 🏠

This little ⬤ had 🍖

This little ⬤ had none,

And this little ⬤ cried "Wee, wee, wee"

All the way 🏠

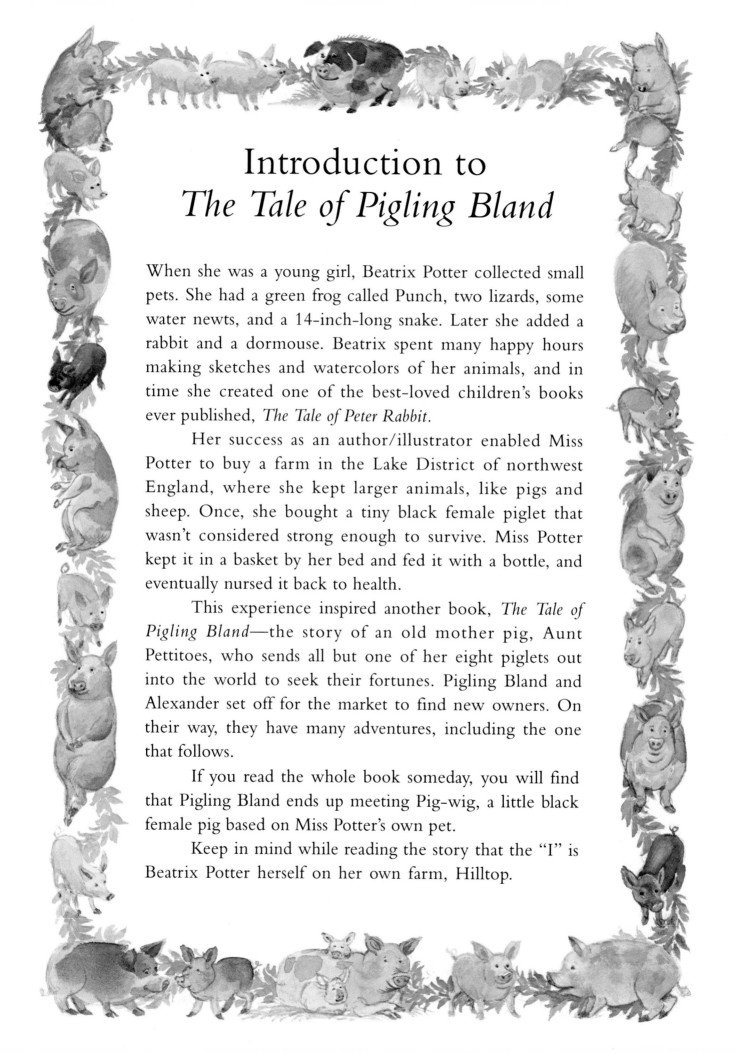

Introduction to
The Tale of Pigling Bland

When she was a young girl, Beatrix Potter collected small pets. She had a green frog called Punch, two lizards, some water newts, and a 14-inch-long snake. Later she added a rabbit and a dormouse. Beatrix spent many happy hours making sketches and watercolors of her animals, and in time she created one of the best-loved children's books ever published, *The Tale of Peter Rabbit*.

Her success as an author/illustrator enabled Miss Potter to buy a farm in the Lake District of northwest England, where she kept larger animals, like pigs and sheep. Once, she bought a tiny black female piglet that wasn't considered strong enough to survive. Miss Potter kept it in a basket by her bed and fed it with a bottle, and eventually nursed it back to health.

This experience inspired another book, *The Tale of Pigling Bland*—the story of an old mother pig, Aunt Pettitoes, who sends all but one of her eight piglets out into the world to seek their fortunes. Pigling Bland and Alexander set off for the market to find new owners. On their way, they have many adventures, including the one that follows.

If you read the whole book someday, you will find that Pigling Bland ends up meeting Pig-wig, a little black female pig based on Miss Potter's own pet.

Keep in mind while reading the story that the "I" is Beatrix Potter herself on her own farm, Hilltop.

from

The Tale of Pigling Bland

story and pictures by Beatrix Potter

"Aunt Pettitoes, Aunt Pettitoes! you are a worthy person, but your family is not well brought up. Every one of them has been in mischief except Spot and Pigling Bland."

"Yus, yus!" sighed Aunt Pettitoes. "And they drink bucketfuls of milk; I shall have to get another cow! Good little Spot shall stay at home to do the housework; but the others must go. Four little boy pigs and four little girl pigs are too many altogether.

"Yus, yus, yus," said Aunt Pettitoes, "there will be more to eat without them."

So Chin-chin and Suck-suck went away in a wheelbarrow, and Stumpy, Yock-yock and Cross-patch rode away in a cart.

And the other two little boy pigs, Pigling Bland and Alexander, went to market. We brushed their coats, we curled their tails and washed their little faces, and wished them good-bye in the yard.

Aunt Pettitoes wiped her eyes with a large pocket hand-kerchief; then she wiped Pigling Bland's nose and shed tears; then she wiped Alexander's nose and shed tears; then she passed the handkerchief to Spot. Aunt Pettitoes sighed and grunted, and addressed those little pigs as follows:

"Now Pigling Bland, son Pigling Bland, you must go to market. Take your brother Alexander by the hand. Mind your Sunday clothes, and remember to blow your nose"—(Aunt Pettitoes passed round the handkerchief again)—"beware of traps, hen roosts, bacon and eggs; always walk upon your hind legs." Pigling Bland, who was a sedate little pig, looked solemnly at his mother, a tear trickled down his cheek.

Aunt Pettitoes turned to the other—"Now son Alexander take the hand"—"Wee, wee, wee!" giggled Alexander—"take the hand of your brother Pigling Bland, you must go to market. Mind—"

"Wee, wee, wee!" interrupted Alexander again. "You put me out," said Aunt Pettitoes—"Observe signposts and milestones; do not gobble herring bones—" "And remember," said I impressively, "if you once cross the county boundary you cannot come back. Alexander, you are not attending. Here are two licenses permitting two pigs to go to market in Lancashire. Attend, Alexander. I have had no end of trouble in getting these papers from the policeman." Pigling Bland listened gravely; Alexander was hopelessly volatile.

I pinned the papers, for safety, inside their waistcoat pockets; Aunt Pettitoes gave to each a little bundle, and eight conversation peppermints with appropriate moral sentiments in screws of paper. Then they started.

Pigling Bland and Alexander trotted along steadily for a mile; at least Pigling Bland did. Alexander made the road half as long again by skipping from side to side. He danced about and pinched his brother, singing—

"This pig went to market, this pig stayed at home,

This pig had a bit of meat—

"Let's see what they have given *us* for dinner, Pigling?"

Pigling Bland and Alexander sat down and untied their bun-

dles. Alexander gobbled up his dinner in no time; he had already eaten all his own peppermints. "Give me one of yours, please, Pigling." "But I wish to preserve them for emergencies," said Pigling Bland doubtfully. Alexander went into squeals of laughter. Then he pricked Pigling with the pin that had fastened his pig paper; and when Pigling slapped him he dropped the pin, and tried to take Pigling's pin, and the papers got mixed up. Pigling Bland reproved Alexander.

But presently they made it up again and trotted away together, singing—

"Tom, Tom, the piper's son,

stole a pig and away he ran!

But all the tune that he could play

was 'Over the hills and far away!'"

"What's that, young sirs? Stole a pig? Where are your licenses?" said the policeman. They had nearly run against him round a corner. Pigling Bland pulled out his paper; Alexander, after fumbling, handed over something scrumply—

"Two 2½ oz. conversation sweeties at three farthings"— "What's this? This ain't a license." Alexander's nose lengthened visibly; he had lost it. "I had one, indeed I had, Mr. Policeman!"

"It's not likely they let you start without. I am passing the farm. You may walk with me." "Can I come back too?" inquired Pigling Bland. "I see no reason, young sir; your paper is all right." Pigling Bland did not like going on alone, and it was beginning to rain. But it is unwise to argue with the police; he gave his brother a peppermint, and watched him go out of sight.

To conclude the adventures of Alexander—the policeman sauntered up to the house about tea time, followed by a damp subdued little pig. I disposed of Alexander in the neighborhood; he did fairly well when he had settled down.

Pigling Bland went on alone dejectedly; he came to cross-roads and a signpost—"To Market Town, 5 miles," "Over the Hills, 4 miles," "To Pettitoes Farm, 3 miles."

Pigling Bland was shocked; there was little hope of sleeping in

Market Town, and tomorrow was the hiring fair; it was deplorable to think how much time had been wasted by the frivolity of Alexander.

He glanced wistfully along the road towards the hills, and then set off walking obediently the other way, buttoning up his coat against the rain. He had never wanted to go; and the idea of standing all by himself in a crowded market, to be stared at, pushed, and hired by some big strange farmer was very disagreeable—

"I wish I could have a little garden and grow potatoes," said Pigling Bland.

I Had a Little Pig

I had a little pig,
I fed him in a trough,
He got so fat
His tail dropped off.
So I got me a hammer,
And I got me a nail,
And I made my little pig
A brand-new tail.

Anonymous

20

If a Pig Wore a Wig

If a pig wore a wig,
    What could we say?
Treat him as a gentleman,
    And say "Good day."

If his tail chanced to fail,
    What could we do?—
Send him to the tailoress
    To get one new.
          Christina Rossetti

Tale of Five Little Pigs

*Children will have fun acting out the different verses—
curling up, pretending to sleep, and rolling over.
A child or an adult can act as the farmer.*

Moderately fast

Five   lit - tle   pigs   curled   up   in   a   heap,——

Oink,   oink,   oink.   Those   lit - tle   pigs   curled

up   in   a   heap,   They   shut   their   eyes   and

went   to   sleep,——   Oink,   oink,   oink.

2. They slept and slept and slept and slept,
   Sh—sh—sh—
   They slept and slept and slept and slept
   And slept and slept and slept and slept—
   Sh—sh—sh—
3. The farmer woke them one by one
   Oink, oink, oink,
   The farmer woke them one by one
   And then they rolled out in the sun
   Oink, oink, oink.

4. They rolled and rolled and rolled and rolled
   Plop—plop—plop—
   They rolled and rolled and rolled and rolled
   And slept and slept and slept and slept—
   Plop—plop—plop—

5. Those little pigs rolled back in their pen
   Oink, oink, oink,
   Those little pigs rolled back in their pen
   And then they went to sleep again.

The Three Little Pigs

fairy tale retold by Walter Retan
illustrations by S. D. Schindler

Once upon a time there were three little pigs whose mother decided that they should go out into the world to seek their fortunes.

"Just be sure to build your houses before the first frost comes," she warned. "And always mind your manners."

The three little pigs promised to do as their mother told them. Then each set out on a different road.

The first little pig walked along until he met a farmer with a load of hay.

"Please, Mr. Farmer," said the first little pig, "give me some straw to build me a little house."

The farmer gave the first little pig some straw, and the pig built himself a little straw house.

The first little pig had just settled down in his straw house when a wicked wolf came along. The wolf knocked at the door.

"Little pig, little pig," he called, "let me in, let me in!"

"Not by the hair of my chinny chin chin!" answered the first little pig.

"Then I'll huff and I'll puff and I'll blow your house in!" roared the wolf.

But still the first little pig wouldn't let him in. So the wolf huffed and he puffed and he blew the house in.

That was the end of the first little pig.

The second little pig walked along until he met a woodcutter with a cart full of sticks.

"Please, Mr. Woodcutter," said the second little pig, "give me some sticks to build me a little house."

The woodcutter gave the second little pig some sticks, and the pig built himself a house. No sooner had he settled in his little house of sticks than along came the wicked wolf.

"Little pig, little pig," he called, "let me in, let me in!"

"Not by the hair of my chinny chin chin!" answered the second little pig.

"Then I'll huff and I'll puff and I'll blow your house in!" roared the wolf.

And the wolf huffed and he puffed, and he puffed and he huffed, and at last he blew the house in.

That was the end of the second little pig.

26

The third little pig walked along until he met a bricklayer with a wagon full of bricks.

"Please, Mr. Bricklayer," said the third little pig, "give me some bricks to make me a little house."

The bricklayer gave the third little pig some bricks, and the pig built himself a house. But he was barely settled in his little brick house when along came the wicked wolf.

"Little pig, little pig," the wolf called, "let me in, let me in!"

"Not by the hair of my chinny chin chin!" answered the third little pig.

"Then I'll huff and I'll puff and I'll blow your house in!" roared the wolf.

Well, he huffed and he puffed, and he puffed and he huffed, and he huffed and he puffed, but he could *not* blow the house in.

As he turned away in anger, the wolf muttered to himself, "Just you wait. I'll catch you another way."

Soon the wolf was back at the little pig's door.

"Oh, little pig," he called in his friendliest voice, "I know where there is the nicest field of turnips."

"Where?" asked the little pig.

"In Farmer Brown's garden," answered the wicked wolf. "If you will meet me there at six o'clock tomorrow morning, I will show you where the juiciest turnips grow."

The next morning the little pig got up at *five* o'clock and hurried to Farmer Brown's garden. By the time the wolf came, at six, the little pig was snug and safe at home again, cooking his turnips on the stove.

The wicked wolf was very angry when he discovered this. "Little pig, little pig, I'll catch you yet," he muttered to himself.

Sure enough, the wolf was soon back at the little pig's door.

"Little pig," he called, "if you will meet me in Farmer Brown's orchard at five o'clock tomorrow morning, I will show you the tree that has the sweetest apples."

The next morning the little pig got up at *four* o'clock and hurried to Farmer Brown's orchard. But he was still up in one of the apple trees when he saw the wolf coming along, down below.

"My, my," said the wolf, who was sure he had trapped the little pig at last. "You got here ahead of me again. Are the apples as tasty as I promised?"

"Yes, very," said the little pig. "I will throw one down to you."

But he threw the apple so hard that it rolled down the hill and the wolf had to go running after it. While the wolf was running, the little pig jumped down and ran home with his basketful of apples.

But the wolf was not ready to give up. The very next day he was back at the little pig's door.

"Little pig," he called, "tomorrow there is a fair in the village. If you will meet me there at three o'clock, I will show you the best things to buy."

But the next day the little pig got to the fair at *two* o'clock and bought himself a new barrel. He was just starting home with it when he saw the wolf coming up the hill.

Quickly the little pig jumped into the barrel to hide. The barrel suddenly began to roll down the hill, *thumpety-thump*, with the little pig squealing inside. The wolf was so frightened by the squealing runaway barrel that he ran straight home.

The next day, when the wolf discovered that he had been fooled again, he was very angry indeed. He declared that he would eat the little pig if it was the last thing he did.

He climbed right up on the little pig's roof and called down the chimney, "Get ready, little pig, for I am coming down the chimney to eat you up."

As soon as the little pig heard what the wolf was doing, he took the lid off a huge pot of water that was bubbling on the fire. Down tumbled the wolf—right into the boiling water. The little pig popped the cover back onto the pot, and that was the end of the wicked wolf.

As for the little pig, he lived happily ever after.

Three Little Pigs and a Little Pig More

Three little pigs and a little pig more
Hold up three fingers; then another to make four.
Knocked on the farmer's bright green door:
Knock loudly on the floor.
"Be quick, Mr. Farmer, we want our lunch,
Hunch, hunch, hunch!"

Three little calves and a little calf more
Hold up three fingers; then another to make four.
Knocked on the farmer's bright green door:
Knock loudly on the floor.
"Be quick, Mr. Farmer, we want our lunch too,
Moo, moo, moo!"

The farmer came out with a furious roar:
"Who's that a-hammering at my door?
Not a bit, not a scrap will you get from me."
Thus said he.
Those poor little animals knocked once more,
Quietly, quietly on the door,
Knock quietly on the floor.
And said most politely on their knees,
"If you please!"

33

Pig Builds a House

traditional folktale
illustrations by Diane de Groat

There was once a pig who thought he hadn't a worry in the world. He lived in a large pigsty with plenty of clean straw for a bed. Every day the farm girl brought him as much food as he could eat, and every day he grew fatter and fatter.

But one day, when the farm girl gave him his food, she said, "You had better eat as much as you can, Mr. Pig, because you won't be here much longer. Tomorrow the farmer is going to kill you and turn you into bacon."

The pig kept eating until every single bit of food was gone. Then he gave a loud snort, butted open the pigsty door with his big snout, and ran off to the neighboring farm.

There he went straight to the sheepfold, to visit a sheep he had often met out in the field. When he saw the sheep, he greeted him warmly.

"Good day to you, too," answered the sheep. "Indeed I am in good health, thank you. What brings you here to my farm?"

"Do you know why your master feeds you and makes you so comfortable?" asked the pig.

"No," answered the sheep.

"Because when you are big enough and fat enough, he is going to kill you and eat you," said the pig.

"Well, I don't think I want that to happen," said the sheep. "But what can I do?"

"Just come with me," said the pig. "We'll run off to the woods where our masters can't find us. There we'll build us a house that will be both safe and comfortable."

The sheep was happy to run away with the pig. "Good company is a fine thing," he said. "And a long life is even better."

The two of them set off in the direction of the woods. They had not gone far before they met a goose.

"Good day, good sirs," said the goose. "And where might you be going today?"

"Good day to you, too," answered the pig. "We just learned that our masters were fattening us up so they could eat us. But we're not stupid enough to let that happen. We're running away to the woods to build us a house."

"May I go with you?" asked the goose. "You will find that the work is much easier if there are three of us to share it."

"And what can you do to help us build a house?" asked the pig.

"I can pull grass and stuff it in the cracks between the logs," answered the goose. "That will make your house tight and warm."

Above all, the pig wanted to be warm and comfortable, so he agreed that the goose could join the group.

They had not gone far before they met a rabbit who came frisking out of the meadow.

"Good day, sirs, and where might you be traveling?" asked the rabbit.

"Good day to you, too," answered the pig. "We found that our masters were not to be trusted, so we are running off to the woods to build us a house. As you probably know, there is nothing like having a home of your own."

"That is very true," said the rabbit. "I tell my friends that I have a home in every bush. But when winter comes, a bush isn't enough. Then I always promise myself that if I just live until summer, I'll build me a real house."

"Well, you could come with us," said the pig. "But I don't know what you could do to help."

"There is always something for a good worker to do," said the rabbit. "I have teeth to gnaw pegs and strong paws to drive them into the wall. I can be your carpenter."

The pig decided that a carpenter would be useful, so he invited the rabbit to join his group.

When they had gone a little farther, they met a rooster.

"Good day, good sirs," said the rooster, "and where are you going today?"

"Good day to you, too," answered the pig. "We are running off to the woods to build us a house."

"Well," said the rooster, "that is just the sort of thing that I would like to do. Could I join you?"

"And how could you help us to build our house?" asked the pig.

"Well, now," answered the rooster, "since I am always the earliest riser, I can wake everybody else up with my crowing."

"Very true," said the pig. "By all means, come along with us."

So all five of them set off to the woods to build a house. The pig cut down the wood, and the sheep pulled it home. The rabbit gnawed out pegs and bolts and hammered them into the walls and the roof. The goose pulled up grass and stuffed it into the cracks. And the rooster crowed loudly every morning to make sure the others didn't oversleep.

Soon the house was ready. They lined the roof with birch bark and covered it with heavy sod. And there they lived, happy and comfortable without a worry in the world.

"'Tis good to travel east and west," said the pig, "but there's no question—home is best."

As I Looked Out

As I looked out on Saturday last,
A fat little pig went hurrying past.
Over his shoulders he wore a shawl,
Although it didn't seem cold at all.
I waved at him, but he didn't see,
For he never so much as looked at me.

Once again, when the moon was high,
I saw the little pig hurrying by;
Back he came at a terrible pace,
The moonlight shone on his little pink face,
And he smiled with a smile that was quite content.
But never I knew where that little pig went.

Anonymous

Tom, Tom, the Piper's Son

Tom, Tom, the pi - per's son, Stole a pig and a -

way he run; The pig was eat And

Tom was beat, And Tom went howl - ing down the street.

The Very Long Trip

from TALES OF AMANDA PIG

by Jean Van Leeuwen
pictures by Ann Schweninger

"What can we do on a rainy day?" asked Amanda. "You could do puzzles," said Mother. "All the puzzles have pieces missing," said Oliver. "Amanda ate them when she was a baby."

44

"You could read books," said Mother.

"I've read them all," said Amanda. "Let's go to Grandmother's house."

"Not today," said Mother. "It is a long trip and it is raining too hard."

"We could take you in our airplane," said Oliver.

"In that case," said Mother, "I would be happy to go."

Oliver and Amanda got the airplane ready for takeoff. Mother climbed into the backseat.

"Hold on," said Oliver. "We're taking off."

There was a loud noise.

"What was that?" asked Mother.

"The engine," said Oliver. "I think something is broken."

He took his screwdriver and lay down next to the airplane. "It's fixed now," he said.

The airplane flew for a few minutes.

"Lunchtime!" said Amanda. She climbed out of the airplane.

"You can't get out," said Oliver. "We are flying in the air."

"Oh," said Amanda. She climbed back in.

Oliver landed the airplane.

"Let's sit in the grass and have a picnic," said Amanda.

"What are we having?" asked Mother.

"Chocolate chip sandwiches," said Amanda. "And raisins for dessert."

They had their picnic.

"Now it's my turn to be the driver," said Amanda.

The airplane flew some more.

"Are we almost there?" asked Mother.

"Yes," said Amanda.

There was a terrible noise.

"What was that?" asked Mother.

"We landed on Grandmother's roof," said Amanda. "But we didn't break it."

"Hello, Grandmother," said Oliver. "Well, we have to go now. Good-bye."

"That was a short visit," said Mother.

"We can't stay all night," said Amanda. "We forgot our toothbrushes."

They flew home.

"Look," said Mother. "The rain has stopped."

Oliver and Amanda looked outside. There was Grandmother coming up the front walk.

"Grandmother!" said Amanda. "We wanted to visit you but it was raining too hard. So we flew to your house in our airplane."

"I wanted to visit you too," said Grandmother. "And here I am."

"It was a very long trip," said Oliver.

"Yes, it was," said Grandmother. "But I'm glad I came."

"Me too," said Amanda.

The Book of Pigericks

written and illustrated by Arnold Lobel

There Was a Light Pig from Montclair

There was a light pig from Montclair.
Dressed in feathers, she floated on air.
When the birds saw her frock,
They called, "Come, join our flock!"
Which she did, in the skies of Montclair.

There Was a Small Pig Who Wept Tears

There was a small pig who wept tears
When his mother said, "I'll wash your ears."
As she poured on the soap,
He cried, "Oh, how I hope
This won't happen again for ten years!"

The Princess
and the Pig

Turkish folktale retold by Walter Retan
illustrations by John Wallner

In far-off Turkey there was once a sultan who had three daughters. All three princesses were very beautiful, but the youngest was the loveliest of all.

One day, when the sultan was about to set off for town, he asked his daughters if he could bring them anything from the market.

"I would like a golden gown," said the oldest daughter.

"And I would like a silver sash," answered the second daughter.

But the youngest said she wanted nothing at all.

"Come now," said her father, "there must be something you would like."

"Well, if you feel you must bring me something, Father, I would like:

Grapes that speak,
Apples that smile,
And apricots that tinkle in the breeze."

Her two older sisters laughed out loud. They had never heard of anything so silly. But their father just smiled.

The sultan had no trouble finding a golden gown and a silver sash, but though he looked everywhere, he could not find any of the things his youngest daughter had asked for.

Finally it was time to return home. He stepped into his carriage, and off the horses went in the direction of the palace.

They were not far from the palace when the carriage suddenly stopped. The wheels were stuck in deep, sticky mud. Though the horses pulled and pulled, the carriage didn't move an inch.

"What do we do now?" thought the discouraged sultan. All of a sudden, from outside, he heard a loud *oink, oink* and a noisy *grumph, grumph*. Looking out the carriage window, the sultan saw an ugly old pig slopping through the mud. He had never before seen such a filthy animal.

"*Grumph, grumph*," grunted the pig. "I can push you out of the mud."

"Well, then, stop talking and start pushing," said the sultan.

"*Grumph, grumph*," said the pig. "First you must promise me your youngest daughter for my bride."

The sultan could not believe his ears. Marry his daughter to a pig? Never! Still, he couldn't stay there in the mud all day. He would deal with the marriage nonsense later!

"Very well," said the sultan, "you may marry my youngest daughter. But right now I would like to see you get my carriage out of the mud."

With just one push of his snout, the pig jolted the carriage out of the mud. The sultan drove off at once without even a thank-you to the ugly pig.

When the sultan arrived at the palace, his two oldest daughters were delighted with their presents.

"Aren't you sorry you asked for such silly presents?" they asked their younger sister. But she didn't in the least mind that her father hadn't been able to find the things she had requested. As for the sultan, he had already forgotten about his promise to the ugly pig.

But late that afternoon they heard a *grumph, grumph* at the door. The pig had come to collect his bride.

The sultan had no choice but to tell his youngest daughter about the promise he had made.

"Well, a promise is a promise," said the good-natured young princess. "I shall just have to go off with him."

The pig grunted happily as he tucked her into his rickety wheelbarrow. The sultan watched them bumping along the road.

"There goes my daughter—about to marry a pig," he said with a sigh. "And to think that this has come about just because my carriage was stuck in the mud."

The pig took his young princess home to his dirty, old tumbledown pigsty. There he gave her some corn for her dinner and a pile of straw for her bed.

The princess was a good-tempered girl, so she didn't fuss about her new home even though she had been used to living in a beautiful palace. She ate her corn, then curled up in the straw. Crying softly, she finally fell asleep in her rough bed.

When the princess awoke, she couldn't imagine where she was. She was lying on a feather bed with sheets of softest silk, and her bedroom was larger and more beautiful than her bedroom at the palace. As she looked about her in astonishment, she saw a handsome young man standing in the doorway.

"Good morning," he said. "This is my palace and you shall be my queen. When I became king a wicked sorcerer cast an evil spell on me, turning me into a pig. Only one thing would undo the spell. I had to marry a girl who asked for:

Grapes that speak,
Apples that smile,
And apricots that tinkle in the breeze.

If you come into my garden with me, you will see the very presents you asked for."

The princess followed her young king down a narrow staircase to a large garden.

"Good morning, my queen," said a bunch of grapes hanging from a vine. Then the princess discovered apples smiling at her from every bough of the apple tree. And farther away, golden apricots tinkled whenever a breeze disturbed them.

The princess had never been so happy! That very morning she and her handsome young king drove off to her father's palace. The sultan was overjoyed to hear the good news. He decreed that a splendid wedding should be celebrated for forty days and forty nights.

When the two older princesses saw their younger sister with her handsome husband, they decided that she hadn't asked for such silly presents after all.

Higglety, Pigglety, Pop!

Higglety, pigglety, pop!
The dog has eaten the mop;
 The pig's in a hurry,
 The cat's in a flurry,
Higglety, pigglety, pop!

Samuel Goodrich

58

Mary Middling

Mary Middling had a pig,
Not very little and not very big,
Not very pink, not very green,
Not very dirty, not very clean,
Not very good, not very naughty,
Not very humble, not very haughty,
Not very thin, not very fat;
Now what would you give for a pig like that?

Rose Fyleman

Poinsettia
& Her Family

story and pictures by Felicia Bond

Poinsettia had six brothers and sisters, a mother, and a father.

They lived in a fine, old house surrounded by hydrangea bushes and lilac hedges, which Poinsettia's mother would occasionally cut for a nice effect in the dining room.

There was pachysandra in which to play hide-and-seek in the early evenings of summer, and a rock out front to sit on.

Inside, there was a red leather window seat for reading in the late afternoon sun, and a bathroom with balloon-pink wallpaper. Poinsettia thought it a perfect house.

One day, Poinsettia came home from the library with her favorite book, a book about a little, spotted circus horse who danced. Poinsettia had read it five times before, but she was looking forward to it all the same. She trotted past her mother in the garden and her father in the kitchen, and headed straight for the red leather window seat. If the sun was coming in the window just right, it would spread like warm butter across the pages of her book. Poinsettia walked a little faster, patting her pocket to make sure it held the cherry tart she had bought for just this occasion.

The sun was coming in the window just right, but it was spreading like warm butter across the fat, little body of Julius, the third from the youngest, who was already curled up on the soft red leather.

"I will go to the rock in the front yard," Poinsettia grunted, "where I can read my book in peace."

But the rock could hardly be seen for all the piglets lying about. "Like a bunch of seals," Poinsettia snorted.

She stomped off toward the balloon-pink bathroom, where the tub was just right for reading. But there, up to her chins in water, was Chick Pea, who said she hadn't washed her feet yet.

"This house would be perfect except for one thing," Poinsettia fumed. "There are too many of us in it! It is not possible to go anywhere without running into a brother or a sister, a mother or a father!"

That night, Poinsettia was very nasty. She pinched a brother, stepped on a sister, and yelled louder than both of them put together. She did more things and worse things, and it was only seven o'clock. Poinsettia was sent to bed early that night for general misbehavior.

The next day, Poinsettia's father announced to the whole family that they were moving. "We will look for a new house," he said. "This one is too small for us."

"Oh, no, it's not," Poinsettia thought. "It's the family that's too big." But she kept her thoughts to herself and vowed not to go with them.

When the family left, Poinsettia lay low in the pachysandra. Nobody noticed. The car seemed full.

She lay there a long time, just in case they came back. They didn't.

"Good," Poinsettia said and, clutching her book close to her, ran straight for the red leather window seat.

The light had never been more buttery, nor the leather as warm. Poinsettia read two pages there, then ran to the rock in the front yard.

The rock had never felt more solid. Poinsettia read six more pages. But a wind was whipping up, and it was even starting to snow.

Poinsettia ran inside.

She warmed herself in a deliciously hot bath. She read four pages, then spent an hour staring dreamily at the wallpaper. It had never looked pinker, and neither had Poinsettia.

"I'm a pig in bliss," she gurgled.

Poinsettia let the water out of the tub.

The snow came down harder, and Poinsettia fell asleep. She dreamed about the dancing circus horse.

It snowed all that afternoon and into the evening. By the time it was dark, Poinsettia had read her book eighteen times. She wrapped herself in an old blanket and looked for something to eat. What little food there was she ate cold.

"The house is not as it used to be," she said aloud quietly. "What I need is a rope! If I had a rope, I could make a tent with this blanket. I could tie the rope to two doorknobs and put the blanket over it. My tent would be a house inside a house. What a good idea."

Poinsettia searched everywhere for a bit of rope. All she found was a frayed piece of string that was barely long enough for anything.

But in the farthest corner of a dark, dark closet, Poinsettia found something else. It was a photograph, an old photograph of her family. Poinsettia remembered taking it herself.

This was too much for Poinsettia. With the point of her hoof, she very carefully made a little hole in the top of the photograph. Through the hole she threaded the string she had found. On each end she made a knot.

"This is all I have left of my family!" Poinsettia cried, and cried, and cried.

"Poinsettia!" a small voice called. "Poinsettia!"

Poinsettia nearly fainted dead away.

There were her six brothers and sisters, her mother and her father, all squashed and crowded together and smiling from ear to ear!

"We would have been back sooner," Poinsettia's father said, "but the car got stuck in the snow. It's a good thing there are so many of us. We all got out and pushed."

"Pierre counted everyone, but he counted wrong because he's only three," said Petunia, the oldest.

"I don't know why we didn't notice right away that you were missing," Julius said, "because everything was so peaceful."

"The whole time we were gone, Poinsettia," her mother said, "we talked about what a wonderful house this is. It is our home. Perhaps we don't need as much room as we thought."

"Maybe not," Poinsettia said.

And shoulder to shoulder, elbow to elbow, all squashed and crowded together, they spent the rest of that night, and many other nights together. . . as together as nine pigs could be . . . in their fine, old house.

A Pig Tale

Poor Jane Higgins,
She had five piggins,
And one got drowned in the Irish Sea.
Poor Jane Higgins,
She had four piggins,
And one flew over the sycamore tree.
Poor Jane Higgins,
She had three piggins,
And one was taken away for pork.
Poor Jane Higgins,
She had two piggins,
And one was sent to the Bishop of Cork.
Poor Jane Higgins,
She had one piggin,
And that was struck by a shower of hail,
So poor Jane Higgins,
She had no piggins,
And that's the end of my little pig tale.

James Reeves

70

Pigs and Pirates

folktale from the Tyrrhenian Sea retold by Walter Retan

A very long time ago, three young friends lived on a small island in the Tyrrhenian Sea, just off the coast of Italy. The boys' names were Franco, Angelo, and Piero, and they watched over a herd of pigs that belonged to a prince on the mainland.

Once a week the prince sent a ship across the water with food supplies for the young swineherds. And once a week the ship carried back two or three of the fattest pigs to be roasted in the royal kitchen.

The three boys led a very happy life on their little island. They climbed trees, swam in the sparkling blue sea, or sat in a cool cave telling stories about bold pirates who roamed the seas.

Once in a while the young swineherds had to chase after runaway pigs or rescue an unlucky pig that had tumbled into a rocky crevice. But the boys had learned that the pigs were really quite smart. They had even taught the pigs tricks. For instance, the pigs had learned to run to the sandy side of the island whenever the boys blew three high notes on their pipes. A special treat was always waiting there for them. Sometimes the treat was a pile of acorns. At other times it was a heap of juicy apples or bunches of golden grain.

But that was not all! Franco had taught one of the cleverest pigs to walk backward on its hind legs. Angelo had trained another to dance a little jig. And Piero had shown a third pig how to lie down on the ground and play dead.

One day a terrible thunderstorm came roaring across the island. Lightning flashed, trees bent almost double, and the rain came down in torrents. Franco, Angelo, and Piero herded all of the pigs into a warm, dry cave overlooking the sea. Then the boys stood at the mouth of the cave, spellbound by the fury of the storm. They

had never seen such high waves or heard such loud claps of thunder.

Suddenly they spied a ship nearby tossing and turning in the wild, frothing waves. Its strange black sails whipped back and forth, driven by the powerful gusts of wind. While the boys watched, a bright flash of lightning struck the ship's mast, splintering it into small pieces. Then a mountainous wave lifted the vessel and carried it right toward the island's rocky cliffs. The boys were certain it would crash against the rocks, but somehow the ship's crew managed to steer it safely into the harbor.

The storm ended almost as quickly as it had blown up. The sky cleared and the ship's crew came out on deck to inspect the damage. From the safety of their cave, the boys studied the strange ship.

Suddenly Franco whispered, "I think it must be a pirate ship! Look at the skull and crossbones on the flag."

"Only pirates would have black sails," said Angelo.

"If we aren't careful, they will steal our pigs and take us prisoner," Piero warned.

"They will never find our pigs if we keep them hidden here in the cave," said Franco.

The three swineherds drove the squealing pigs farther back into the cave. Then they heaped a pile of stones in front of the entrance so that the pirates wouldn't discover it. The three specially trained pigs were hidden separately in another, smaller cave.

"We'd better hide in a tall tree," said Angelo, "so we can spy on the pirates."

Soon the pirates rowed ashore in a longboat. *Tramp, tramp, tramp*, they poked about the island, looking here, there, and everywhere. Before long they had discovered the heap of stones piled in front of the cave. As they started to push the stones to one side, they heard a frightened pig squeal.

"Ho, ho!" shouted the pirate captain. "I hear a pig. That would make a tasty morsel for our dinner!"

The pirates entered the cave and soon discovered the herd of pigs. They wasted no time driving them down to the shore. There they loaded the pigs—pink ones, black ones, and even spotted ones—into their longboat and rowed them out to the pirate ship.

They might never have found the three cleverest pigs in their special hiding place if the pigs hadn't been so curious. As soon as they heard the squealing from the rest of the herd, they wanted to see what was going on. Out came the first clever pig walking backward on its hind legs. Next came the second clever pig dancing a jig.

"There may be others hiding in that cave," said the pirate captain, and he went in to see for himself. He found the third pig lying on the ground, looking as if it were dead. He poked at it with his finger. "It's still warm," he shouted. "We'll have this one for dinner."

From their hiding place in the tree, the three boys watched the pirates row off with their pigs.

"We should have taught our pigs more useful tricks," said Franco.

"A trick that could have saved them from the pirates," added Angelo.

But Piero didn't agree. "I think there *is* a way to save them," he said. "Do you have your pipes?" His friends nodded, wondering what Piero had in mind.

"Follow me," Piero ordered.

Together they climbed quietly down from the tree, then crept through the bushy trees until they reached the sandy shore. Now they could hear the pigs squealing and see them running wildly around the deck of the pirate ship.

"Take your pipes and play our special signal," said Piero. All three boys put their pipes to their mouths and began to blow the three high notes they used to call the pigs for a special treat.

When the boys stopped blowing, they no longer heard the pigs squealing. Had they heard the signal? Once again the boys blew the same clear high notes.

Suddenly all the pigs ran toward the side of the ship that was nearest to the sandy shore. The pirates chased after them, worried that the pigs might get out of control.

Now all the weight was on one side of the ship. Slowly it began to tip over on its side. Then the water rushed over the deck and the ship began to sink.

Right away the pigs started to paddle toward shore as fast as they could go. They were in a hurry to get their special treat.

But the pirates, alas, had never learned to swim. Like most pirates, they were actually afraid of water. Before long, there was nothing left of the pirate ship and its crew except a ring of big bubbles in the sea.

Franco, Angelo, and Piero were so happy to have their pigs back that they gave them a very special feast of acorns, apples, *and* golden grain. And for many days afterward the boys laughed at the trick their smart pigs had played on the evil pirates.

The story spread through all the islands of the Tyrrhenian Sea until it became a legend that is still told today.

The
End

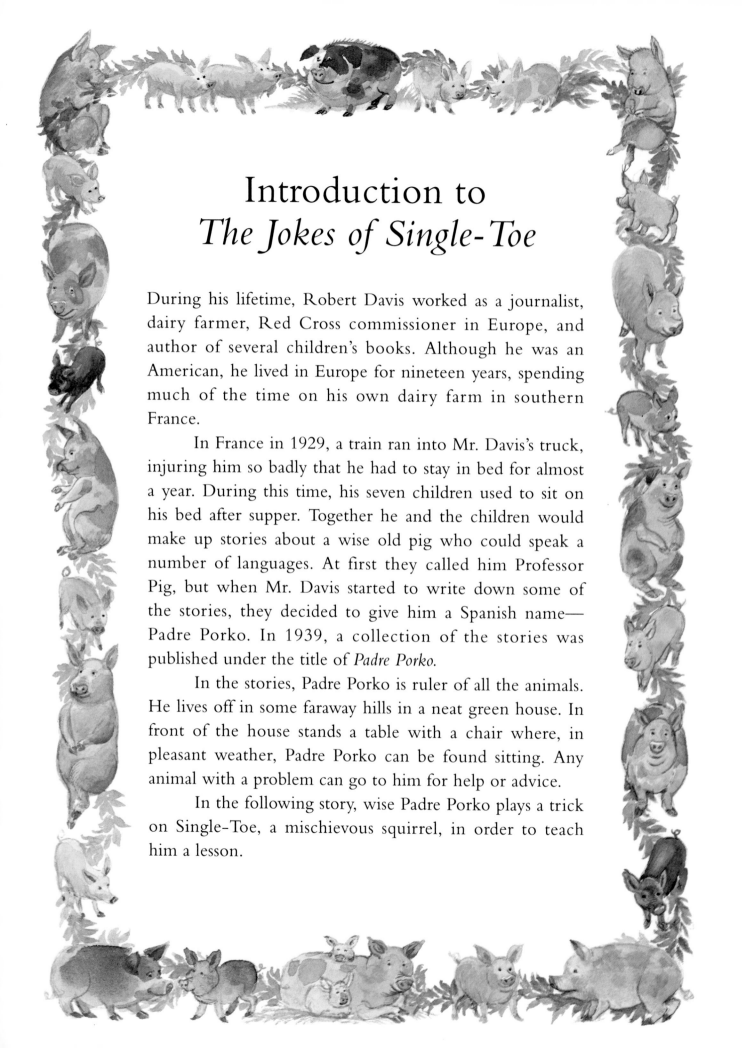

Introduction to
The Jokes of Single-Toe

During his lifetime, Robert Davis worked as a journalist, dairy farmer, Red Cross commissioner in Europe, and author of several children's books. Although he was an American, he lived in Europe for nineteen years, spending much of the time on his own dairy farm in southern France.

In France in 1929, a train ran into Mr. Davis's truck, injuring him so badly that he had to stay in bed for almost a year. During this time, his seven children used to sit on his bed after supper. Together he and the children would make up stories about a wise old pig who could speak a number of languages. At first they called him Professor Pig, but when Mr. Davis started to write down some of the stories, they decided to give him a Spanish name— Padre Porko. In 1939, a collection of the stories was published under the title of *Padre Porko*.

In the stories, Padre Porko is ruler of all the animals. He lives off in some faraway hills in a neat green house. In front of the house stands a table with a chair where, in pleasant weather, Padre Porko can be found sitting. Any animal with a problem can go to him for help or advice.

In the following story, wise Padre Porko plays a trick on Single-Toe, a mischievous squirrel, in order to teach him a lesson.

The Jokes of Single-Toe

from PADRE PORKO

by Robert Davis
illustrations by John Wallner

*A squirrel who is a prankster learns a lesson from
Spain's great animal hero, Padre Porko.*

"Chestnuts are ripening and falling on the other side of the canal," said the black-headed sparrow, teetering on the edge of the table.

"Oh, but it's too early for chestnuts," observed the Padre. "It takes two or three frosty nights to open the prickles."

"Well, if you can't believe me," said the sparrow, ruffling his collar, "ask the squirrel. He keeps track of the nuts."

So the Padre asked Single-Toe (so named because he had only one on his left front foot). The squirrel put his paw beside his nose as though he were trying to think up an answer to a riddle. "I'll try to let you know in three days," he mumbled, "but don't do anything about chestnuts until you see me again." And he went off in such a rush that even the good Padre grew suspicious.

An hour later he laid down his pipe and beckoned to Mrs. Wren. "Do you mind having a little fly around the wood to see what the squirrel family is up to this morning?"

She came back twittering all over. "The squirrels, for miles around, are all in the grove across the canal, throwing down the chestnuts for dear life. Single-Toe is making them work all the harder, and giggling at something he seems to think very funny."

"Oh, the rascal," chuckled the Padre. "The sly little one-toed sinner! He will give me an answer in three days, will he? Yes, indeed, after he has gathered all the best nuts." He called to his housekeeper. "Mrs. Hedge-Hog, bring me three of the oatmeal sacks from the cupboard and some strong string." And folding the bags inside his belt, he trotted off, pushing his wheelbarrow.

81

Up among the leaves, busy pulling the polished nuts out of the burrs, Single-Toe and his relatives did not hear the Padre arrive. Patter, plop, plop, plop, patter—the brown nuts were falling on the grass.

"What a lark," beamed the Padre, stuffing four or five into his mouth at once. "And this year they are sweeter and juicier than they have been for a long time." He made little piles of the biggest ones, and began filling his sacks. Finally he had all the wheelbarrow would carry. Bouncing the last bag up and down so he could tie the string around the top, he called out in his silkiest voice, "Many thanks, Single-Toe. You will see that I have taken only the big ones. I do hope that the prickers haven't made your paws sore."

There was a sudden calm in the chestnut grove. The squirrels came leaping down to a low bough, from where they could send sour looks after the Padre, trundling his barrow along toward the bridge. He was singing,

"With chestnuts roasting in a row,
     I love to hear them sizzle.
I care not how the winds may blow,
     Nor how the rain-drops drizzle.
I welcome every Jack and Jill
     Who knocks upon my door.
We toast our toes and eat our fill,
     For there are plenty more."

83

One day three or four weeks later the Padre was doing a little carpentering under the umbrella pine, when something behind him sniffed. He jumped, and dropped two nails out of his mouth. There, under the table, tears running down their noses, were Mrs. Single-Toe and the four children.

"Bless my blue-eyed buttons," exclaimed the Padre, spitting out the rest of the nails. "What can be as wrong as all that?"

"It's Papa," said the oldest boy. "He's been in a hole by the old oak for four days, and is almost starved."

"But why doesn't he come home?" said the Padre. "The oak isn't far away."

"The fox won't let him," sobbed Madame Single-Toe.

"And why not?"

"He's mad because of Papa's jokes," the youngest child explained.

The Padre's mouth opened in a wide grin. "More of the jokes that other people don't find funny, eh? Well, I'll take a stroll by the twisted oak and have a talk with the fox." As he started off, he called over his shoulder, "Mrs. Hedge-Hog, you might give these youngsters a couple of the pickled chestnuts we keep for company." He winked solemnly at Mrs. Single-Toe, who blushed.

The fox was lying with his muzzle just an inch from the hole. He did not budge, nor lift his eye when the Padre wished him good morning. "I've got him this time," he snarled. "Four days I've been watching this hole. My mother brings my meals and keeps guard while I eat. He'll not get away *this* time!"

"He is a nuisance with his jokes, I admit," said the Padre peaceably, "but he doesn't do any real harm. Don't you think a good scare would be enough for him?"

"No, I don't," snapped the fox. "And don't you mix in this business, Padre, with your talk about kindness. What I've suffered from that little pest you'd never believe. First he dropped a tomato on my nose—a tomato that was too ripe. And then he dribbled pitch all over my head and neck while I was asleep. So don't waste your time." The fox advanced his red tongue hungrily to the very edge of the hole.

The Padre walked away, deep in thought. His generous heart was very unhappy. What should he say to the near-orphans in his kitchen? There must be some way to save him. Suddenly he saw some crows gossiping in a dead pine. "Will one of you birds do me a favor, in a great hurry?" he called.

"Certainly, Don Porko," they all cawed.

"Fly low through the woods and tell every rabbit you see that I want their road commissioner to come to my house for dinner. Say that I'm going to have celery root and cabbage, chopped in parsley."

The Padre's guest was promptness itself. He used a turnip leaf as a napkin, and when he had wiped his whiskers, ate the napkin.

"It makes less for Ma'am Hedge-Hog to clear up," he explained.

"Now for serious business," said the Padre, leading the way to the garden, when they had finished their second glass of dandelion wine. "I have invited you here as an expert. We will draw a map." He made a cross in the soft earth with a stick. "Here is the oak that the lightning split. And here in front of it, so, is a rabbit hole that was begun, but never finished. Do you follow me?"

The road commissioner nodded. "I know it perfectly. The workman was caught by an owl when he came up with some dirt."

"Now," continued the Padre, "how far is the bottom of this unfinished hole from one of your regular tunnels, and how long would it take to dig up to it?"

"About half a jump," replied the road commissioner. "The 'Alley to the Ivy Rock' runs very close to that unfinished hole. A good digger can do a medium-sized jump of tunnel in half a day. I should say it would take two hours to dig upwards from 'Ivy Rock Alley' and join the hole."

The Padre beckoned the road commissioner to follow him to the cellar. Scraping away the sand, he laid bare ten carrots, each as smooth and straight as an orange-colored candle. "These are yours, Mr. Commissioner, if you will do this little job of digging for me."

The bargain was soon struck. "One thing more," said the Padre, as the commissioner was lolloping away. "You will find a friend of mine in the unfinished hole. Don't let him make a noise, but bring him here the moment you can get him free. I'll be waiting."

Daylight was fading when the rabbit returned, covered with damp earth to his armpits. He was supporting a hoarse, hungry, and grimy red squirrel. The Padre welcomed them, pointing to the cupboard. "Sh-h-h-sh, go and see what's inside, Single-Toe."

One might have thought a hundred squirrels were behind the cupboard door, such was the hugging and chattering, the rubbing of noses, and the scratching of ears. Single-Toe was invited to stay for a light lunch, even after the road commissioner had left for his burrow, the biggest carrot in his mouth.

Safe, fed, and warmed, the red squirrel became his own gay self again. He began to chuckle, then to shake with merriment. "Ha, ha, ha! That silly old fox is still there, watching an empty hole! Won't it be a priceless joke if I climb the oak and drop a rotten egg on his nose?"

At the word "joke," Mrs. Single-Toe, the four little squirrels, and the good Padre all stiffened.

"Don't you ever say that word again," said his wife. "Do you hear, no more jokes, never, never."

Single-Toe wilted. "Yes," he confessed, not daring to meet the Padre's eye, "jokes aren't always so terribly funny, are they? Not even for the joker."

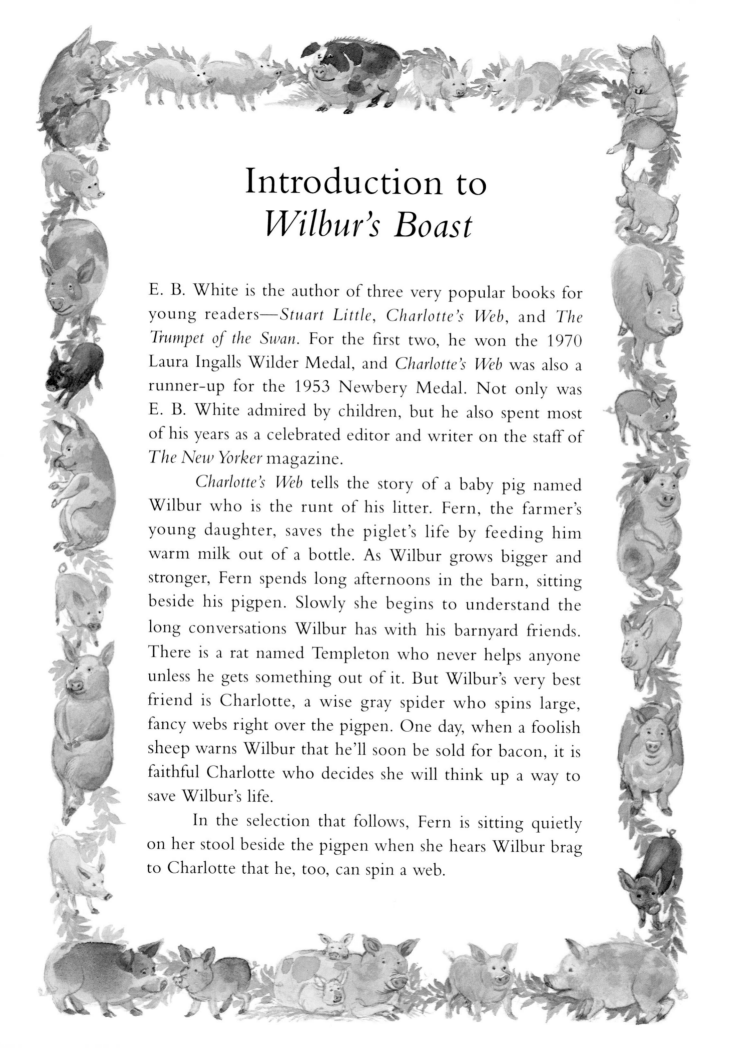

Introduction to
Wilbur's Boast

E. B. White is the author of three very popular books for young readers—*Stuart Little*, *Charlotte's Web*, and *The Trumpet of the Swan*. For the first two, he won the 1970 Laura Ingalls Wilder Medal, and *Charlotte's Web* was also a runner-up for the 1953 Newbery Medal. Not only was E. B. White admired by children, but he also spent most of his years as a celebrated editor and writer on the staff of *The New Yorker* magazine.

Charlotte's Web tells the story of a baby pig named Wilbur who is the runt of his litter. Fern, the farmer's young daughter, saves the piglet's life by feeding him warm milk out of a bottle. As Wilbur grows bigger and stronger, Fern spends long afternoons in the barn, sitting beside his pigpen. Slowly she begins to understand the long conversations Wilbur has with his barnyard friends. There is a rat named Templeton who never helps anyone unless he gets something out of it. But Wilbur's very best friend is Charlotte, a wise gray spider who spins large, fancy webs right over the pigpen. One day, when a foolish sheep warns Wilbur that he'll soon be sold for bacon, it is faithful Charlotte who decides she will think up a way to save Wilbur's life.

In the selection that follows, Fern is sitting quietly on her stool beside the pigpen when she hears Wilbur brag to Charlotte that he, too, can spin a web.

Wilbur's Boast

from CHARLOTTE'S WEB

by E. B. White
illustrations by Garth Williams

A spider's web is stronger than it looks. Although it is made of thin, delicate strands, the web is not easily broken. However, a web gets torn every day by the insects that kick around in it, and a spider must rebuild it when it gets full of holes. Charlotte liked to do her weaving during the late afternoon, and Fern liked to sit nearby and watch. One afternoon she heard a most interesting conversation and witnessed a strange event.

"You have awfully hairy legs, Charlotte," said Wilbur, as the spider busily worked at her task.

"My legs are hairy for a good reason," replied Charlotte. "Furthermore, each leg of mine has seven sections—the coxa, the trochanter, the femur, the patella, the tibia, the metatarsus, and the tarsus."

Wilbur sat bolt upright. "You're kidding," he said.

"No, I'm not, either."

"Say those names again, I didn't catch them the first time."

"Coxa, trochanter, femur, patella, tibia, metatarsus, and tarsus."

"Goodness!" said Wilbur, looking down at his own chubby legs. "I don't think *my* legs have seven sections."

"Well," said Charlotte, "you and I lead different lives. You don't have to spin a web. That takes real leg work."

"I could spin a web if I tried," said Wilbur, boasting. "I've just never tried."

"Let's see you do it," said Charlotte. Fern chuckled softly, and her eyes grew wide with love for the pig.

"O.K.," replied Wilbur. "You coach me and I'll spin one. It must be a lot of fun to spin a web. How do I start?"

"Take a deep breath!" said Charlotte, smiling. Wilbur breathed deeply. "Now climb to the highest place you can get to, like this."

Charlotte raced up to the top of the doorway. Wilbur scrambled to the top of the manure pile.

"Very good!" said Charlotte. "Now make an attachment with your spinnerets, hurl yourself into space, and let out a dragline as you go down!"

Wilbur hesitated a moment, then jumped out into the air. He glanced hastily behind to see if a piece of rope was following him to check his fall, but nothing seemed to be happening in his rear, and the next thing he knew, he landed with a thump. "Ooomp!" he grunted.

Charlotte laughed so hard her web began to sway.

"What did I do wrong?" asked the pig, when he recovered from his bump.

"Nothing," said Charlotte. "It was a nice try."

"I think I'll try again," said Wilbur cheerfully. "I believe what I need is a little piece of string to hold me."

The pig walked out to his yard. "You there, Templeton?" he called. The rat poked his head out from under the trough.

"Got a little piece of string I could borrow?" asked Wilbur. "I need it to spin a web."

"Yes, indeed," replied Templeton, who saved string. "No trouble at all. Anything to oblige." He crept down into his hole, pushed the goose egg out of the way, and returned with an old piece of dirty white string. Wilbur examined it.

"That's just the thing," he said. "Tie one end to my tail, will you, Templeton?"

Wilbur crouched low, with his thin, curly tail toward the rat. Templeton seized the string, passed it around the end of the pig's tail, and tied two half hitches. Charlotte watched in delight. Like Fern, she was truly fond of Wilbur, whose smelly pen and stale food attracted the flies that she needed, and she was proud to see that he was not a quitter and was willing to try again to spin a web.

While the rat and the spider and the little girl watched, Wilbur climbed again to the top of the manure pile, full of energy and hope.

"Everybody watch!" he cried. And summoning all his strength, he threw himself into the air, headfirst. The string trailed behind him.

But as he had neglected to fasten the other end to anything, it didn't really do any good, and Wilbur landed with a thud, crushed and hurt. Tears came to his eyes. Templeton grinned. Charlotte just sat quietly. After a bit she spoke.

"You can't spin a web, Wilbur, and I advise you to put the idea out of your mind. You lack two things needed for spinning a web."

"What are they?" asked Wilbur, sadly.

"You lack a set of spinnerets, and you lack know-how. But cheer up, you don't need a web. Zuckerman supplies you with three big meals a day. Why should you worry about trapping food?"

Wilbur sighed. "You're ever so much cleverer and brighter than I am, Charlotte. I guess I was just trying to show off. Serves me right."

Templeton untied his string and took it back to his home. Charlotte returned to her weaving.

"You needn't feel too bad, Wilbur," she said. "Not many creatures can spin webs. Even men aren't as good at it as spiders, although they *think* they're pretty good, and they'll *try* anything. Did you ever hear of the Queensborough Bridge?"

Wilbur shook his head. "Is it a web?"

"Sort of," replied Charlotte. "But do you know how long it took men to build it? Eight whole years. My goodness, I would have starved to death waiting that long. I can make a web in a single evening."

"What do people catch in the Queensborough Bridge—bugs?" asked Wilbur.

"No," said Charlotte. "They don't catch anything. They just keep trotting back and forth across the bridge thinking there is something better on the other side. If they'd hang head-down at the top of the thing and wait quietly, maybe something good would come along. But no—with men it's rush, rush, rush, every minute. I'm glad I'm a sedentary spider."

"What does sedentary mean?" asked Wilbur.

"Means I sit still a good part of the time and don't go wandering all over creation. I know a good thing when I see it, and my web is a good thing. I stay put and wait for what comes. Gives me a chance to think."

"Well, I'm sort of sedentary myself, I guess," said the pig. "I have to hang around here whether I want to or not. You know where I'd really like to be this evening?"

"Where?"

"In a forest looking for beechnuts and truffles and delectable roots, pushing leaves aside with my wonderful strong nose, searching and sniffing along the ground, smelling, smelling, smelling . . ."

"You smell just the way you are," remarked a lamb who had just walked in. "I can smell you from here. You're the smelliest creature in the place."

Wilbur hung his head. His eyes grew wet with tears. Charlotte noticed his embarrassment and she spoke sharply to the lamb.

"Let Wilbur alone!" she said. "He has a perfect right to smell, considering his surroundings. You're no bundle of sweet peas yourself. Furthermore, you are interrupting a very pleasant conversation. What were we talking about, Wilbur, when we were so rudely interrupted?"

"Oh, I don't remember," said Wilbur. "It doesn't make any difference. Let's not talk any more for a while, Charlotte. I'm getting sleepy. You go ahead and finish fixing your web and I'll just lie here and watch you. It's a lovely evening." Wilbur stretched out on his side.

Twilight settled over Zuckerman's barn, and a feeling of peace. Fern knew it was almost suppertime but she couldn't bear to leave. Swallows passed on silent wings, in and out of the doorways, bringing food to their young ones. From across the road a bird sang "Whippoorwill, whippoorwill!" Lurvy sat down under an apple tree and lit his pipe; the animals sniffed the familiar smell of strong tobacco. Wilbur heard the trill of the tree toad and the occasional slamming of the kitchen door. All these sounds made him feel comfortable and happy, for he loved life and loved to be a part of the world on a summer evening. But as he lay there he remembered what the old sheep had told him. The thought of death came to him and he began to tremble with fear.

"Charlotte?" he said softly.

"Yes, Wilbur?"

"I don't want to die."

"Of course you don't," said Charlotte in a comforting voice.

"I just love it here in the barn," said Wilbur. "I love everything about this place."

"Of course you do," said Charlotte. "We all do."

The goose appeared, followed by her seven goslings. They thrust their little necks out and kept up a musical whistling, like a tiny troupe of pipers. Wilbur listened to the sound with love in his heart.

"Charlotte?" he said.

"Yes?" said the spider.

"Were you serious when you promised you would keep them from killing me?"

"I was never more serious in my life. I am not going to let you die, Wilbur."

"How are you going to save me?" asked Wilbur, whose curiosity was very strong on this point.

"Well," said Charlotte, vaguely, "I don't really know. But I'm working on a plan."

"That's wonderful," said Wilbur. "How is the plan coming, Charlotte? Have you got very far with it? Is it coming along pretty well?" Wilbur was trembling again, but Charlotte was cool and collected.

"Oh, it's coming all right," she said, lightly. "The plan is still in its early stages and hasn't completely shaped up yet, but I'm working on it."

"When do you work on it?" begged Wilbur.

"When I'm hanging head-down at the top of my web. That's when I do my thinking, because then all the blood is in my head."

"I'd be only too glad to help in any way I can."

"Oh, I'll work it out alone," said Charlotte. "I can think better if I think alone."

"All right," said Wilbur. "But don't fail to let me know if there's anything I can do to help, no matter how slight."

"Well," replied Charlotte, "you must try to build yourself up. I want you to get plenty of sleep, and stop worrying. Never hurry and never worry. Chew your food thoroughly and eat every bit of it, except you must leave just enough for Templeton. Gain weight and stay well—that's the way you can help. Keep fit, and don't lose your nerve. Do you think you understand?"

"Yes, I understand," said Wilbur.

"Go along to bed, then," said Charlotte. "Sleep is important."

Wilbur trotted over to the darkest corner of his pen and threw himself down. He closed his eyes. In another minute he spoke.

"Charlotte?" he said.

"Yes, Wilbur?"

"May I go out to my trough and see if I left any of my supper? I think I left just a tiny bit of mashed potato."

"Very well," said Charlotte. "But I want you in bed again without delay."

Wilbur started to race out to his yard.

"Slowly, slowly!" said Charlotte. "Never hurry and never worry!"

Wilbur checked himself and crept slowly to his trough. He found a bit of potato, chewed it carefully, swallowed it, and walked back to bed. He closed his eyes and was silent for a while.

"Charlotte?" he said, in a whisper.

"Yes?"

"May I get a drink of milk? I think there are a few drops of milk left in my trough."

"No, the trough is dry, and I want you to go to sleep. No more talking! Close your eyes and go to sleep!"

Wilbur shut his eyes. Fern got up from her stool and started for home, her mind full of everything she had seen and heard.

"Good night, Charlotte!" said Wilbur.

"Good night, Wilbur!"

There was a pause.

"Good night, Charlotte!"

"Good night, Wilbur!"

"Good night!"

"Good night!"

A Pig Is Never Blamed

A pig is never blamed in case
he forgets to wash his face.
No dirty suds are on his soap,
because with soap he does not cope.
He never has to clean the tub
after he has had a scrub,
for whatever mess he makes,
a bath is what he never takes.
But then, what is a pool to him?
Poor pig, he never learns to swim.
And all the goodies he can cram
down his gullet turn to ham.
It's mean:
keeping clean.
You hardly want to, till you're very big,
But it's worse to be a pig.

Babette Deutsch